dave roman
astronaut academy
Zero Gravity

:01

First Second

New York & London

This **FORGED** symbol of instructional excellence was bestowed upon me by the power of the Intergalactic Educational Advisory Board and the local P.T.A.!

I also got this crafty robotic arm-- just one of the perks of tenure.

NOW! Let's start making points! We all know that the future of education is in **OUTER SPACE!**

WHY!?

GASP!

But that does not mean you should **RANDOMLY** be sent spiraling into that oxygen-devoid vacuum.

So don't choose a sub-par facility where you are hypothetically forced to share chalk with co-students who don't take themselves seriously or who sleep in late.

SPACE BUS

You owe it to the **FUTURE** of yourself to choose **NOW!**

Only ASTRONAUT ACADEMY IS tops...

WITH the LEARNING!

Your parents will be sitting back home trusting in our **ALLEGED** educated expertise.

A diverse curriculum means
MANY CLASSES TO CHOOSE!

ADVANCED HEART STUDIES!   **ANTI-GRAVITY GYMNASTICS!**

WEARING CUTE HATS!   **FIRE THROWING!**

RUN-ON SENTENCES!   **LOCKER!**

AND SEVERAL OTHERS.!!! (without illustrated examples)

If dominating test scores is as important to _YOU_ as it is to _MY SWORD_, then you'll love that our teachers are on _PAYROLL!_

LIKE: Mrs. Bunn

Who is old enough to know so many answers to _QUESTIONS!_
(YOU MIGHT BE IMPRESSED!)

AND: Mr. Namagucci

SCIENCE WITH YOU

Who may or may not have magical powers but is still _HANDSOME!_
(ASK AROUND!)

AS WELL AS: Señor Panda

HOLA AMIGOS

A brand new _ADDITION_ to our faculty!
(STILL NOT EXTINCT!)

Here is an authentic student who has parents with enough *PULL* to get her into this promo...

I'm *SO RICH* I don't even *NEED* an education!

But I still opt to go here just for the thrill of being the **BEST!**

OKAY! Now you know the full extent of *HOW GOOD* it is to be attending ASTRONAUT ACADEMY!

WELCOME ASTRONAUT AC

GO!

So prepare for the after effects that come from being *SO* knowledgeable!

But don't forget to arrange for someone to *PICK YOU UP* for winter break!

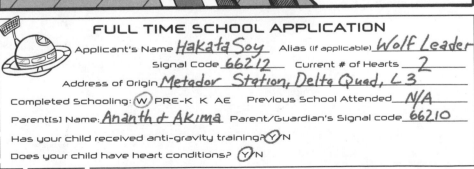

FULL TIME SCHOOL APPLICATION

Applicant's Name _Hakata Soy_   Alias (if applicable) _Wolf Leader_

Signal Code _66212_   Current # of Hearts _2_

Address of Origin _Metador Station, Delta Quad, L3_

Completed Schooling: (W) PRE-K K AE   Previous School Attended _N/A_

Parent(s) Name: _Ananth & Akima_   Parent/Guardian's Signal code _66210_

Has your child received anti-gravity training? (Y) N

Does your child have heart conditions? (Y) N

astronaut academy

first semester

It's easy to focus on how cold and lonely
a **SPACE** the galaxy can be.

Especially when you are
by *YOURSELF.*

And the bus driver has cranked up the *AIR CONDITIONER!*

Speak up if you need me to adjust the comfort levels.

But I must *CONDITION MYSELF* for *HARSH ENVIRONMENTS...* if I expect to survive the next few months.

Adapt to the *CLIMATE OF CHANGE...* because where I'm headed I know I will be *TESTED.*

SPACE BUS

So kid, you got a name?

HAKATA SOY

★ はかた ★

ASTRONAUT ACADEMY

Bit *LATE* for classes that started over a month ago-- don't ya think?

T ACADEMY

I've been *TIED UP.*

Captive in our arch-rival's basement the whole time!

Good thing you were able to signal us with your communicom device!

Heh-heh. I can certainly relate.

It's so easy to get distracted when you are *FLYING* by like time!

WHOOSH

LEVEL
3

And since you are unrecognizable to me, you must be the student who is **SUPPOSED** to be new here.

I am a resident advisor, which most people abbreviate as **R.A.** to save on letters!

Full name is Debbie, but I go by "D" for short people, who refer to me as **R.A.D.** once they know what's up above them. **HOTCHA!**

This paper seems nice and **OFFICIAL**-- which I like to see in documents.

Looks like you'll be staying in **DORMROOM X.**

I hope you fit in and don't try to cause trouble, okay?

FOOSH

Oh. You're **FINALLY** here.

I thought I was going to have to wait up **ALL YEAR!**

It will take a lot of *ADJUSTING* to get used to this new life.

Even though we are floating in the *OUTER SPACE*, this school does not feel like my place in the universe. I can't help but feel *LOWER* to the ground.

But I shall attempt to fall into some *SLEEP* for I know it is needed by my body to avoid becoming *WEAK.*

And sleep is what activates *DREAMS,* which is where my *COMFORT* comes to visit me in my tired mind.

WOO HOO!

HIPPITY HOP HOORAY! ♪♫

METADOR! YOU SAVED OUR CITY FROM UTTER DESTRUCTION AND STUFF!

THE END!

My name is:

DOUG HIRO

And I go to:

ASTRONAUT ACADEMY

Walking in space is fun and easy to like.

Being upside down is the best way to see your feet.

weeeeeeee

The vastness of space...

...is *ETERNAL.*

THE
END!

Well, that only makes me **MORE** curious...but I won't push the issue since teaching math is a higher calling than my casual interest in **CHARACTER PROFILING.**

You can take that empty seat between Miyumi San and Marcos Stamatis.

I hope I don't place your life in any **DANGER** by sitting here.

Back to the subject of this class. Let's start **ADDING** two and two together by solving these **QUESTIONABLE EQUATIONS!**

$2+2=X$
$X+33-CAKE$

TO THE POWER OF Y?

TWO MINUTES LATER...

TAP TAP

SNAP!

. . .

UMMM...

Pencil sharpener?

WHEW!
THANKS!

Us NEIGHBORS have to look out for each other!

SALUTE

?

END!

My name is: **MIYUMI SAN** みゆみ♡♡ and I go to: **ASTRONAUT ACADEMY**

Okay class, today begins your **DINOSAUR DRIVING LESSONS!**

BOOORINNG. I've been driving dinosaurs since kindergarten.

Blah! That Maribelle Mellonbelly **SO** plays the snob role.

I guess it **PAYS** since she's the daughter of a wealthy business tycoon.

Well, rich people often make **BIG MISTAKES.** I would love to see her fall on her face, which is smug.

Oh, Miyumi! You are so mean, but in the **BEST WAY**-- which is fun!

Enough jibber-jabber! It's time to pick your dinosaurs. Hurry before they become extinct-- **AGAIN!**

31

YES! I AM THE SMARTEST AND FASTEST GIRL IN ALL ASTRONAUT ACADEMY! BASK IN MY GLOWING GLORY!!!

This makes no sense! I thought GOOD was supposed to prevail?

I can't believe that I could be such a LOSER.

NOT SO FAST! Just because Maribelle crossed the finish line first, that does not make her a TRUE WINNER.

WHAT?! HOW CAN THIS BE?!

Nope. You see, class, Maribelle forgot the MOST IMPORTANT PART of Dinosaur Driving! Wearing your CUTE LITTLE HAT!

Which is why Miyumi wins the race and gets an A+ for being SMART.

SLURP

HOORAY! Justice is served--FRESH!

PHOTO FINISH!

And *HOW* do you know him *EXACTLY*? You're not an ex-girlfriend *ARE YOU?!* I hope *NOT*, cuz that would mean you are now *MY ENEMY*.

BACK OFF, SISTER!

EAT!

NO! It is *NOTHING* like that conclusion you have jumped to in *COMPLETE INACCURACY!*

My story is less *ROMANCE-BASED* and instead, rather *HEROIC!*

WINK

OH, GOOD! Then I will enjoy listening to it *MORE* now that we are clear that I have *NO REASON* to envy you.

A few years ago on the far off planet of Hoppiton.

I lived hoppily with my family in a peaceful city.

Greetings, Meta-Team! This is Wolf Leader, do you *READ ME?*

Loud and clear, captain! What seems to be the trouble that *ONLY WE* can put a stop to?

Bunnies under *ATTACK* from some foreign invaders dressed like *BIRDS* with lasers!

Sounds like the *FREAKS* who go by the moniker

Them *AGAIN?* They are so close to becoming *RECURRING VILLAINS* who *KEEP* showing up at bad times.

FOOLS! What do they gots against bunnies? Don't they know how *CUTE* they are? Especially when they *HOP* around.

Good point. And I love those *LONG EARS* and the way they eat the *CARROTS.*

That's why we have to stop those birds before there's *NO BUNNIES LEFT!* Somebody's got to have *COTTON TAILS* and eat those *HEALTHY SNACKS!*

END!

My name is:

DOUG HIRO And I go to: ASTRONAUT ACADEMY

 Doug Hiro! Won't take off his helmet in class! Please give him a *DETENTION* or something comparable because he should really know better.

Teacher! You aren't going to let him keep being *SO WEIRD...* am I right?! And it's giving me a *CONDITION!*

 Space excercises are over, so can you please *REMOVE* the helmet over your head so we can begin class without distraction?

 But... ...I don't wanna.

 SEE! Remember when I told you he was a freak who did things that could be considered weird to normal kids like *US?*

He probably can't hear you because his ears are *COVERED* with helmet.

 Yeah, or they are *FILLED* to the brim with dumbness.

If he likes space so much we should shoot him out of the airlock.

 Woo hoo! AIRLOCK!

 Sit back down, Mr. Hiro. There are restrictions against shooting students out of the airlocks.

 AWWWW!

 Someday... SWOOSH

end!

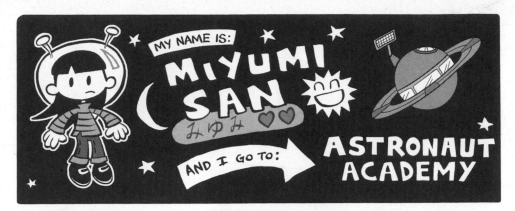

My name is: MIYUMI SAN みゆみ

And I go to: ASTRONAUT ACADEMY

Today's Adventure

BOY ALERT!

This is BILLY LEE.

He thinks he is the HOT STUFF.

Probably because he has a big POMPADOUR.

So he thinks he can get a date just because he ASKS?

Hey, Baby!

MANLY WIGGLE

OH, GROSS!

NO!

WHAT? HEY! WATCH THE THREADS!

OH! I GET IT! You don't want to be my girlfriend because my hair intimidates you. It's UNDERSTANDABLE.

UMM... NO...

It's just that...

It's just that I... already HAVE a man. SPIKE JOHANSON! WOO HOO!

WHO? WHAA?

HA! I am **SO** not believing that story that it is making me laugh, **HA!**

HA HA HA

Everyone knows that Spike is more fond of people who are **BOYS!**

And not only that but he **ALSO** particularly fancies hunks with **WELL-GROOMED** hair!

I like what I like.

FINE!

Well, good thing I dumped that deadbeat and traded him in for a **SPACE MONKEY!**

PLOP

Space monkey? Is that **LEGAL???** Well, I guess I can't compete with that.

DARN RIGHT! Monkeys know how to treat a lady.

Excuse me, Miss San...

...but we need the monkey back for class.

53

MY NAME IS: **BILLY LEE** AND I GO TO: ASTRONAUT ACADEMY

Last week, if an interviewer asked me:

What do you think is your **STRONGEST QUALITY?**

I'd have to say the hair.

Which would have been redundant since my hair always spoke for **ITSELF.**

But due to the sensitive nature of **CURRENT EVENTS...** I'd probablty now opt to focus on:

My ability to love.

IMAGINARY PRESS CONFERENCE

And if in a **SPECULATIVE EXPOSÉ** there was a question about what **USED** to be my favorite subject of school, I would have **ORIGINALLY** said:

HUMANITIES WITH PROFESSOR L

For the original weeks of this semester, I was the **ONLY BOY** smart enough to sign up for **HUMANITIES**, a class known for its appeal to girls.

THE LADIES, as I refer to them, are eager to learn about mushy stuff like the inner workings of human hearts.

> Traditionally you start off with only **ONE HEART** and are given 1-2 additional hearts by parents or guardians.

Although money can't buy you love, extra hearts **CAN** be traded or given away as **TOKENS** of affection.

> You gotta love **LOVE**, am I right?

> I'm a **FAN.**

The **GOLDEN AGE** of this class was becoming lab partners with the two most **ANTAGONISTIC** girls in school: **MIYUMI SAN** and **MARIBELLE MELLONBELLY!**

57

The time was *RIPE* for making a *FRESH* start if I ever wanted to find myself in a *FRUITFUL* relationship. So I asked my dad for advice.

No girl can refuse a son of mine!

REALLY?

Refreshed my knowledge of the *WOO.*

*OH...*It's all about *FIRST* impressions!

I must have originally skipped this chapter.

MACHO 101

And went from:

HEY...

to:

HEY, BABY!

Which I guess is what lead to:

FIREBALL ACTIVATE!!!

SIZZLE

Things went from **BALD** to **WORSE** once Hakata Soy arrived on the scene.

QUICK!

Get out of here before anyone **SEES** you!

SHOVE

But I'm **REGISTERED** in this class!

NOT WITH THAT COOL HAIR!

Schedule

IT'S NOT MY FAULT!!!

I couldn't argue with his logic. So now the class (which used to be my favorite) has **TWO** guys.

Which gives me less of an **ADVANTAGE** considering my lack of mysterious past or the benefits of being **NEW.**

Hakata immediately struck a bond with Miyumi, which I thought would serve to rile up Maribelle.

We should go on a date to make them jealous.

HMPH. JEALOUS.

But instead she just closed herself off.

Can't you see I'm busy acting like I don't care?

Would you like me to go tell her? Free of charge?

Not worth it.

So, yeah... I guess the *THRILL* is gone. Two of my hearts will always belong to Miyumi and Maribelle and the hatred they have for each other. But if I was asked to go on record, I'd have to confess:

Humanities ain't what it *USED* to be.

HEH.

END!

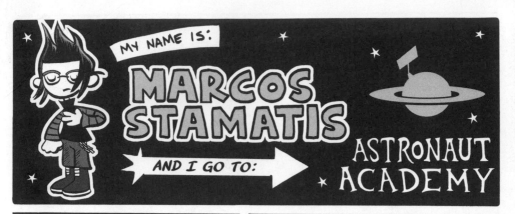

MY NAME IS: **MARCOS STAMATIS** AND I GO TO: → **ASTRONAUT ACADEMY**

For the past few weeks I've been sitting next to this guy Hakata Soy in math class.

He's also in the same *TACTICAL RANDOMNESS WORKSHOP* as me on weekends.

You, sir? Would you like to buy a banana for eating?

If only I were not a sign post.

I may not know the guy's *BACKSTORY*, but I can tell you one thing for certain: someone special must have broken at least one of his hearts.

Oh.

I guess I'll stop bothering you then.

You see, broken hearts are something I know a bit about.

Ever since I got a crush from a girl in my Rocket Science class during first year.

DROP!

OOPS.

I don't know what I saw in her and I *STILL* don't even know her name! Supposedly she was fairly popular, which normally is a huge *TURNOFF* for someone as *ANTI-SOCIAL* as me.

Carry this to the launchpad for me. *NOW!*

Yes, Ma'am!

She was *MEAN* in ways that felt *MEANINGFUL*...or at least *MEANT* something to *ME*.

And *TRY* not to break it!

=SIGH=

I am *SO* not in the mood for this today.

I know that doesn't make much sense...But it didn't matter because it was the first time I was interested in getting to *KNOW* someone else!

Who *IS* that?

Then I had to go and *RUIN IT* by trying to talk to her.

That was pretty awesome how you made those girls cry.

Did I *ASK* for your endorsement?

Having her be *SARCASTIC* right to my face made my heart pound in my chest.

I'd lay awake at night, clenching my chest unable to think about anything but her *SNARKY TONE OF VOICE.*

THUMP
THUMP
THUMP

Eventually *THE BEATING* was unbearable! So in a rash decision, I decided to give my *LONGING HEART* away.

WHAT'S THIS?

Better be good.

A heart container?

From Marcos Stamatis?

TRASH

TOSS

Who's *THAT?*

By the time I managed to retrieve my heart it was *SHATTERED IN TWO.*

I did get it mended...

...but now whenever I *REABSORB* it...

...my body starts to feel *OVERWHELMED* and *OUT OF BALANCE.*

So I've been keeping the unsettled heart underneath my pillow at night.

It's the only way I can keep it close... and still get any sleep.

THUMP

THUMP

THUMP

THUMP

Sorry, I didn't mean to go completely off-topic, but that's my theory about this new kid, Hakata Soy.

Okay, class. Next week we'll focus on being random underwater.

STOP

RIBBIT!

He's trying not to let his past weigh him down. To focus on life here at Astronaut Academy. But all his hearts, just aren't *IN IT*.

META-TEAM HEROES

ARTIFICIAL INTELLIGENCE

The End.

MY NAME IS:

GADGET THOMPSON

AND I **DON'T** GO TO:

ASTRONAUT ACADEMY

I live in a small *ASTEROID SUBURBAN COMMUNITY.* Most of my awake hours are spent in this lab, which belongs to me.

My dad built it when I was a *YOUNGER* kid, and for a while it served as a secret base for me and my friends.

Those were good times...

TUB TYKE BOOTS GADGET HAKATA

SPACE NEWS

5 FRIENDS DEFEAT EVIL MENACE AGAIN!

#1 DEFENDERS OF ROBOT ENFORCED JUSTICE (Proper)

#1

NEWS

HEROES!

...and I have the *TROPHIES* to prove it.

I especially miss Hakata Soy because he was like a brother who **WASN'T RELATED** to me. It's been several long weeks that have passed since his parents sent him off to boarding school **FAR AWAY** from where I live.

BACK IN THE DAY:

But I've been busy cloaking my loneliness by productively building a **NEW FRIEND** to keep me company.

And the significant detail to this robot will be the addition of a **HUMAN HEART**.

A heart that once belonged to Hakata Soy.

THE END!

MY NAME IS: **MIYUMI SAN** みゆみ ♡ AND I GO TO: **astronaut academy**

DRESS TO IMPRESS

Today's Adventure

Why am I such a stereotype?

It's Wednesday and also **11:00 AM**, the time for me to attend my science class!

Te-he! Have fun, because I **KNOW** it is your favorite of the subjects!

Oh, it's **SO TRUE!** I do love **THE SCIENCE.** But it has little to do with education... or things that are often much more fun to **SAY** than do... like "Hydroponics."

In fact, I remember when I didn't even **LIKE** science!

That's back when our teacher was: **THE LAWS OF PHYSICS**

that guy...

But ever since he was replaced by...

$E = mc$

Mr. Namagucci!

I've been riding the **HYPOTHETICAL** wave of passion.

I am not *SHALLOW!* I can date an *OLD PERSON!* What's the big deal?

The "big deal" is that you are a student and he is *YOUR TEACHER!*

So for you to choose *HIM* as your schoolgirl crush would make you a *STEREOTYPE!*

G A S P!

Aww man! I never realized *HOW RIGHT* your points are!

It is predictable! How did I become such a *PARODY* of typical behavior?

Miyumi San, can you answer the question I just asked the class while you were *NOT* paying attention?

No.

You see sir, because you are so handsome, I was *BLINDED* by science.

And since there was no *DEDUCTIVE REASONING,* my experiments in adoration led to *PREDICTABLE* distraction.

So if you don't mind, I'll just go sit in the back of the class and take a failing grade.

CLAP

CLAP

CLAP

♥end♥

My name is: **DOUG HIRO**

And I am: **THE RULER OF OUTER SPACE!**

*Oh, and I guess I go to ASTRONAUT ACADEMY

Today, class, we will be practicing how to assemble satellite equipment in non-atmospheric environments.

You will be judged on your *EXPEDIENCY* and how well you incorporate the *ADVANCED SKILLS* we've practiced during the semester you've had so far.

Any Questions?

Doug?

Can we tumble?

Well, *NORMALLY* I'd say we've done enough tumbling for one semester...

...but since you are wearing that *FANCY CROWN* it sounds like a royal idea.

Hail to the King!

My name is: TAK OFFSKY MVP at: ASTRONAUT ACADEMY

LOOKIT, I'm not an idiot, okay?

I know you're making fun of me.

What makes you think *YOU* are so awesome?

NOTHING, right? So *SAVE IT*.

Besides, I didn't *ASK* to be named "Tak."

MUNCH MUNCH

It was all my parents' idea, so take it up with *THEM*. And if you're going to all the trouble, tell them I said "hi."

I kind of miss them, ya know? It's not easy living so far away from home all semester long.

SPACE BUS

STOP

If I was a *WUSS* or something corny like that kid in that movie with the dog and all the crying, I *MIGHT* get upset from time to time.

But Momma says I gotta be *TOUGH* for her.

And being tough comes *EASY* to me.

So stop *JUDGING* or else I'll *SLUG* you.

Okay, maybe I won't. But that's only because I don't want to ruin my status of being *MOST VALUABLE*. I'd hate to get kicked off the team...

A A
MITCH
FIREBALL
STAR BURGER
CHAMPIONS
ASTRONAUT ACA
CURRENT HEROE

...seeing as how, now, we're considered so *UNBEATABLE*.

Of course, **EVERYONE** wants to be on the team. Especially now that we've started winning some games.

GO SESAME SEEDS!

How is it you can **RULE** so much?

I am TOUCHING!

By **DIVINE RIGHT**, of course!

Everyone **EXCEPT** my "new" roomate.

Hey, do you like Fireball?

Not really.

BUNNY PRIDE

He is **SOOOO** weird.

How can anyone not like Fireball? It is only the **BEST** physical activity **EVER!** And I am saying that because I'm **REALLY, REALLY** good at it-- so I know what I am talking about here.

"MR. CHIBI SESAME SEED SAYS: GO TEAM!

CLASH

0120

Were you at the scrimmage? Did you see that wicked pass?

Sorry, I spent the afternoon studying for mid-terms.

WHAT IS WRONG WITH YOU!?!

I'm just not really **INTO** sports.

I guess we're done talking.

I've been living with Hakata Soy for weeks! And I've confirmed that we do not have **ANYTHING** in common.

How can you eat that stuff?

TOTES of OATS
I gotta bag it up!

Sugar festival
it begins!

It's **TOTE-ly** good for you.

I really know nothing about him and I don't want to take the time to find out.

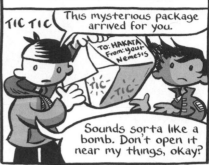

TIC TIC

This mysterious package arrived for you.

TO: HAKATA
From: your Nemesis

TIC -TIC-

Sounds sorta like a bomb. Don't open it near my things, okay?

I'm busy enough as it is. Being on the Fireball team is a full-time commitment. People expect us to be awesome **ALL THE TIME!** But sometimes I just want to take a nap. I guess that's the price of fame. You only get to sleep at night.

Luckily I'm not the **ONLY** shoulder that has to carry the burden.

I've got my fellow Sesame Seeds!

STAR BURGER

I like to refer to them as my "crew" and pretend that we travel the far seas together on **NAUTICAL ADVENTURES!**

Go team!

chibi

S.S. Sesame

In reality, my teammates and I mostly spend our afternoons on the moonroof, looking forward to upcoming tournaments.

We also love to remember how last year's championship game played out!

They thought they were skilled at winning just because they had defeated us so many times.

But last year we *REALLY* practiced making an effort.

FOOSH!

CRACKLE

Yeah, my friends and I pretty much make the best team ever.

And this year's games are going to be even greater.

Couldn't agree more.

Totally.

Same here!

But yesterday I invited them over to my dorm for strategizing and other sophisticated types of things. I should have known my roommate would be there again.

Do you want me out of your way?

Why? You think you're *TOO COOL* for us?

No, I just figured since you *USUALLY* don't like me around.

See what I mean?

He's **ALWAYS** like that!

He does not seem *SO* weird.

Trust me, he gets *WEIRDER!*

A few days ago he asked to use my computer to check all these old message boards.

And get this: I think he even ordered a pair of "Princess Boots."

Princess brand? I never heard of those.

Probably something *ULTRA GIRLY*-- even for you.

I think there is something *MACHO* about a guy who is not afraid to wear ladies' foot wear.

YOU WOULD.

GRR

Can we change the subject back to Fireball before I puke?

☆ The end ☆

I am programmed for: **DESTRUCTION!** A sentient weapon with a singular mission...

SEEK OUT and *ELIMINATE* that goody two-boots, Hakata Soy!

AHEM!

//RANTING MODE INTERRUPTED.//

//HEAT SENSORS ACTIVATED.//

//ANALYSING DNA OF SUBJECT.//

There are no *FIRE BLASTS* permitted in the hallways.

//SCANNING COMPLETE. RESULTS NEGATIVE.//

You are *NOT* Hakata Soy.

Therefore there is no need to **DECIMATE** you. *MOVE ALONG.*

You'd better come with me to the Guidance Chancellor.

Is *THAT* where I can find Hakata Soy?

Because I'm supposed to **ANNIHILATE** him.

Even though my scanners say you are also not Hakata Soy, would you like to still be of use to me?

BLEEP

Prepare me for what to expect from this person of authority. Do they know the location of **SPECIFIC STUDENTS?**

TELL ME...

Boop

COMMUNICATE!

The Chancellor will see you now!

Boop
Beepa!

Oh, hello again, Doug! Did you have an appointment today as well?

Beep

No. Just hanging out.

Okay then, just let us know if you need anything.

Thanks Mrs. Cupcake.

Guidance Chancellor Bee, this is the little *hon* that was found wandering the halls.

Come on in, future success story.

HMM, Cybert, *WOW*. You don't look familiar to me. Have you been to my office before?

//SCANNING FOR ANSWERS//

I'm new.

HOW EXCITING!

But you didn't transfer here from P.S. Gamma Q *DID YOU?*

No, I'm *JUST* completely new.

That's a relief! Kids at that school transfer here just so they can spy on our Fireball team!

Ya know, we had *ANOTHER* student who was new recently. Quiet fellow with dark hair similar to yours. Name escapes me at the moment.

HAKATA SOY?!

No...I think I'd remember a name like *THAT*. I just know he was a bit too sullen, as if reflecting on some past.

But I'm more about what people can *BEE* than what they *WERE*. Speaking of which, what do you hope to do with your life? And would you like a honey-flavored cough drop?

Do with my life? Cough drop? *WELL... UM*, my mission is to hunt down and *DESTROY* Hakata Soy.

OH, MY. That sounds awfully *NEGATIVE*.

And a bit *LIMITING*, don't you think?

Wouldn't you rather do something more *POSITIVE* with the path your life is on?

INSPIRATION NEEDS PERSPIRATION!

How come destroying Hakata Soy wouldn't be positive?

Anything involving "destruction" *CAN'T* be good for you.

How do you know? Have you ever *TRIED?*

I know you kids don't think a guidance chancellor can be *DOWN* with the youth culture, but trust me, I keep up with all the latest *BUZZ!*

So *DIG THIS...* A Hakata Soy is like one of those *ELUSIVE CHARACTERS* in these MonChiChiMon cards all the teachers keep having to *CONFISCATE* during classes.

HE IS?!

GAME CARD

Well, my programming *DOES* say Hakata goes to class...I should keep listening but *START* paying attention.

You could spend your *WHOLE LIFE* searching for an exclusive chase card...

+ 3
- 0

+ 26
- 4

+ 12
- 1

GAME CARD

MCM

+ 9
- 1

+ 9
- 3

+ 8
- 16

CHIM CHIM CHERRIES

DELICIOUS COOKIE DOUGH

DEATH DEALER MONKEY

ARTIFICIAL ARCHITECT

FLAME-TAILED SQUIRREL

TACOMON

...and no matter how many booster packs you buy, never find the one you seek.

Cybert, I want you to look directly into my mask and tell me what you see, okay?

Do you mean *BESIDES* the reflection of myself?

My face, it is like a mirror...

LIKE?

YES! Think about things you *LIKE*... and how these interests shaped your very essence.

Now reach into the *BACKPACK OF YOUR MIND* and shuffle around those earliest memories.

Remember how the world felt?

95

//INFORMATION LOCKED//
//ACCESS DENIED//

Just one last bolt.

It's protecting something *TRAUMATIC* that must have happened to you when you were still in *INFANCY*.

SUCKER PUNCH

I sense *RESISTANCE*. You must have some kind of mental block.

Cybert?

You can stop reflecting now.

HUH?

WHERE I BEE?

You're still in my office. Don't fret the side effects of hypnotism.

Wait...I'm confused... What is my mission again?

We've only just cracked the surface of your childhood.

You'll need a *BREAKTHROUGH* before I can help you figure out who *YOU* really want to bee.

I recommend you take a copy of *MY BOOK*. Read it and swing by after the semester break, so we can continue our progress.

BEEIN' YOURSELF

☆ The end ☆

MY NAME IS: **SCAB WELLINGTON** AND I GO TO: → **ASTRONAUT ACADEMY**

Not that it's any of your business.

But if you must know I just happen (not by chance) to be the friend who is the **BEST** of Maribelle Mellonbelly.

WHAT!? You haven't heard of her, you say?

Then you are a darn **LIAR!**

Because last time I checked (which was **NOT** recently) Maribelle Mellonbelly is the richest and therefore **MOST PROCLAIMED** girl in all of Astronaut Academy!

THE BEST

MARIBELLE MELLONBELLY

Yeah, I **THOUGHT** that might ring a bell.

So how did I get to become best pals with someone so awesome?

But that doesn't mean I ain't afraid to **MILK IT** for all it's worth.

POUND

And yes that **DOES** mean picking on other kids.

Yeah, I like having power over people, so sue me. But I only get *PHYSICAL* against people who deserve it (or have it coming to them).

SMACKING HAND TUCKED AWAY FOR YOUR SAFETY.

Top of that list (yes, there is an actual list) is that no good Miyumi San, who is a *TARGET* because she has a lot of *NERVE* (and that's not just a reflex).

That LIST,
1. MIYUMI
2. CALICO
3. ???
4. THERESA

You may think this guy is some hobo just because he has messy hair and doesn't talk much. But he's really Hakata Soy, who up until recently was *PRETTY NEW.*

VROOM VROOM

And Maribelle likes things that are pretty *AND* things that are new (sometimes both at the same time).

So it makes the sense that he would *ATTRACT HER.*

MAGNETISM

Literally!

OKAY... WEIRD.

She even started to write him a note...

Dear Hakata,

...in her *MIND!*

But then, we found out that Hakata was stupid enough to be friends with someone on that list (see above).

Lee Press-on claws

So now I'm going to have to tear Miyumi's hair out.

Just wait till Spanish class...

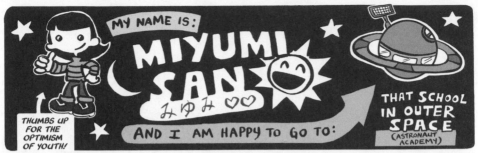

My name is: MIYUMI SAN ☺ みゆみ ♡♡ and I am happy to go to: THAT SCHOOL IN OUTER SPACE (ASTRONAUT ACADEMY)

THUMBS UP FOR THE OPTIMISM OF YOUTH!

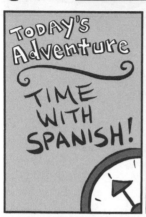

TODAY'S Adventure

TIME WITH SPANISH!

S'OKAY, chicas and chicos!

Today we're going to start reviewing the Spanish that you're **SUPPOSED** to have learned by now.

OY, VEY! Already with the reviewing? Time sure does move fast when you live in the future--like we do. It still feels like yesterday *JUST HAPPENED!* (I can't get over that!)

I should appreciate the moment, instead of *REFLECTING ON THE PAST* like I'm about to...

WOWEE! The first day of classes! *HOW NEW!*

I can't wait for that to happen to me.

It's *HAPPENING* now!

Because I'm giving you this *TIME-BENDING* watch.

Cool, thanks! But if it's not *DIGITAL* how can I tell what time it is?

Well *NORMALLY* you'd just see what numeral this arrow is pointing at. But this watch has been modified to *STOP TIME.*

Too bad. I could sure use a *REGULAR* watch that could help me stop forgetting to *WATCH* my favorite shows.

Well, you *COULD* use this watch to turn back time and tell your past self to watch the shows for you!

FABRIC OF TIME

Drop that taco and turn on channel 832!

QUE WHA?

*YEAH...*but I'm not sure if that would feel the *SAME.*

"If it's all the same to you" is a phrase that will take on *NEW MEANING* once you catch up with me.

106

Obviously, Señor Panda hasn't stuck to the syllabus. But trust me with the authority that comes from being *SLIGHTLY* older; he knows what he's doing.

OKAY... But what if I *FAIL* my final exam?

OH! Don't worry about that because I *ALREADY* took it for you.

You took my Spanish test for me!?

YEP! It's in your future!

I'd feel violated if we weren't the same person!

But Señor Panda doesn't care about proficiency exams or mock lessons.

He only cares about *WHO* is taking them.

≷EEK≷

≷GULP≷

≷SIGH≷

You see, he's trying to find someone.

Because he's not a *REAL* Spanish teacher.

That panda is an *UNDERCOVER AGENT!*

Sent here from the Intergalactic Bureau of Wellbeing.

THIS IS FOR MESSING WITH MY BEST FRIEND, *MARIBELLE MELLONBELLY,* THE RICHEST AND PRETTIEST GIRL IN ALL OF *ASTRONAUT ACADEMY!*

YOU CROSSED THE LINE!!!

...AND NOW I'M GONNA TEAR OUT ALL YOUR *HAIR!*

¡NO WAY, JOSÉ!*

*SPANISH FOR "NO WAY, JOE."

This is so hard to *WATCH!* No one should have to *WATCH* their own hair get pulled out! Oh, Miyumi, *WATCH OUT* for her fork-hand! "Watch" is a word that's spelled the same as...

← THE SWEAT OF FEAR

...WATCH!

It's MISTER watch.

I'm sorry, MR. Watch, can you *STOP TIME,* please?

WATCH ME!

Hey, it worked! They're frozen like characters in a comics panel! Thanks, Mr. Watch!

S'all right.

I just need to carefully pull you off and place my other self away from harm.

I'll take it from here, chica--I mean, Miyumi.

Señor Panda? How come you aren't affected by the power of Mr. Watch?

Because *I'M* the one who gave that watch to your future self.

They're standard issue to officers of the I.B.W. elite, which I am.

I had been *THINKING* of giving it to you so you could help me in my top secret investigation, since you are such a thoughtful person and don't have a criminal record.

Well it looks like you *DID* because here we *ALL* are!

Not for long!

Mr. Watch, please *START TIME* again!

FIZZLE

The Miyumi that was me from the future has **VANISHED!**

YEP.

Once I realized I was going to give you that time control watch, *YOU* became **HER!** And therefore **SHE** no longer needs to exist.

Use this wisely.

AFFIRMATIVE!

A FUTURE EVENT THAT NO LONGER NEEDS TO HAPPEN.

↑
PANDA THOUGHTS

I'm not sure that makes sense... but if my future-self (who has now passed) told me anything PROPHETIC, it was to trust my elders. Especially when they are ME.

Or a panda!

I only wish I had a chance to say goodbye to myself.

UNROLLED CUFFS IN HER HONOR

I'll never forget her.

HEY! What just happened?!

How did I get on the other side of the room? And *SO QUICK!*

There will be plenty of *TIME* to bring you up to speed later. For now I'll be taking you to I.B.W. headquarters for *DETAINMENT.*

Is that like detention plus entertainment?

Take care of Mr. Watch, Miyumi. I'm trusting you to be my right hand, arm-wearing watch man (who is a girl).

AFFIRMATIVE!

Señor Panda?

Is this gonna *ALL* be on the test?

¡AY DIOS MÍO! HA! HA! HA!

★ LOS End ★

My name is:
$MARIBELLE $MELLONBELLY

And I am the richest and most pretty girl in all of...

ASTRONAUT ACADEMY

Can you believe that money *ISN'T* everything?

Sigh...

I know it seems like *CRAZY TALK* the way it sounds so unrealistic.

And I should know since I'm the kind of girl who comes from a family that is *LOADED*...

...WITH CASH!

Even a *LOT* of money is not *ENOUGH* for me anymore.

Sob

Rice isn't sticky enough.

I didn't even know I was *CAPABLE* of a sad expression until a few days ago--when my best friend *DISAPPEARED!*

Have you seen this girl?

Isn't that you?

I meant the kid *BEHIND* me.

I heard that some alien cat thing rode in on rollerblades and bonked her.

RANDOM!

All the rumors that are going around are making me suspicious of *FOUL PLAY*...

...and *FOUL BREATH* as well.

After the panda explained how time travel works he dragged her off to some secret government compound!

ICK! Wash your mouth before you talk!

I like to blame Miyumi San because she is my arch-rival. But accusations do nothing to fill the *EMPTY SPOT* by my side.

☆ The end ☆

Monique, Martin, and Tomcat Are **TEAM FEETY PAJAMAS**

THEY TERRORIZE: → aSTRoNauT academy

Have you ever stared at darkness straight in the FACE!?

LA LA LA

I'm ignoring you.

You cannot ignore the very source of evil, omnipresent!

Watch me. No! You **watch** me! And cower in fear!!

Now... kneel before your new MASTER!!

SHHH!

SHHH, is not a word understood by villains!

Martin, perhaps then you should look up the word "SHHH" in the dictionary section. Also, please don't sit on the floor without a reading mat.

I'm sorry, Ms. Noche...

...but Tomcat *ISN'T.* Bears aren't afraid of authority. They follow their *OWN* laws.

Dark... Scary... Furry... LAWS!

Did it work? Were you able to gather up any minions?

I almost had one in my grasp.

But then I got yelled at by the librarian.

Why is she *ALWAYS* meddling in our affairs!?

114

Were you both just singing?

QUIET PLEASE
⊘
THIS IS A LIBRARY.

WHAT OF IT?

Nothing, I guess.

Just be careful is all.

BUTTER PUP: BOOK OF PIE

WAIT! What are *YOU* doing?

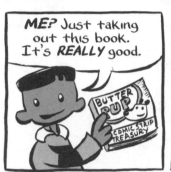

ME? Just taking out this book. It's *REALLY* good.

BUTTER PUP COMIC STRIP TREASURY

Yeah. I *KNOW.* That's why *WE* were going to take it out.

We *WERE?*

YES.

Sweet.

Be sure to bring it back the first week after the break.

You got it, Ms. Noche.

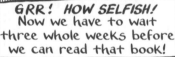

GRR! *HOW SELFISH!* Now we have to wait three whole weeks before we can read that book!

Excuse me, what was that previous customer's name?

Customer? Oh, you mean, *Malik!*

Thanks for *COOPERATING.* You just got back on my good side.

Enjoy that while it lasts, Librarian.

Malik, on the other hand, should consider himself a walking target awaiting retribution from *TEAM FEETY PAJAMAS!!!*

BWA HAHA!!

Shhh!

Oops.

🐻 The end??

116

Did you know my name is: **MALIIK** Mehendale? AND I GO TO: ASTRONAUT ACADEMY

Please pass these little blue test books to the kid who sits behind you.

AHH, YES!

This is what makes it all worthwhile!

Here.

Treasure the moment.

You're supposed to take one and then pass the *REST* back.

RIGHT.

Thanks!

BLUE BOOK

Almost contact ↗

Umm...yeah. No problem.

HEY SPAZOID! Can the rest of us get a booklet too?!

CLUTCH

Or do you need to lick them first?

Malik! Pass those tests BACK!!!

Sigh... These belong to you now.

Ten years later...and DAMPER.

~Whew~ At least I still get to hang on to this one.

BUT for how long?

Soon this test will be over and with it the semester. And with *THAT*, this class, where I have been lucky to have the *BEST VIEW*...

...IN ALL OF MATHEMATICAL HISTORY!

Because I got to sit directly behind Sabrina Spitaro!

She's the girl whose head I know the back of better than my own hand.

practically a stranger (by comparison)

My favorite hour of the day.

Watching her ears poke out through her brown hair.

I sit patiently.

Waiting for those fleeting moments.

Where she might turn even for a *FRACTION*.

...mumble mumble... carry the one... mumble mumble...

Her quarter view like a four leaf clover...

...a complete turn-around like a visit from Halley's Comet.

BLUE BOOK

AHH...good times.

You have 10 minutes before time is UP!

I guess I mastered an understanding of the mathematical arts *AFTER ALL*, because this test was easier *DONE* than studied for.

I'm pretty confident my score will be greater than >expected.

I owe it all to Sabrina and her *ACUTE ANGLES*.

YUM!

If only we could spend *QUANTITATIVE TIME* in some *CONVERSING LINE* or *COMMON DENOMINATOR*. Just me and her equaling a *RECIPROCAL OF ONE*.

WOOP! WOOP!

THAT'S THE SOUND OF THE ALARM! IT IS INTERRUPTING YOUR CLASSES FOR AN EMERGENCY ANTI-GRAVITY DRILL! THIS MAY OR MAY NOT ACTUALLY BE A TEST-- SO TRY NOT TO FREAK OUT, UNLESS WE SAY TO!

HUH? What did that omnipresent voice just say?

It's an anti-gravity drill.

Best day of my life I think.

What about the math exams?

Do they still *COUNT?*

All right now, hand in your booklets to avoid cheating or losing them in a nearby wormhole.

BLUE BOOK

LET'S GO!

I always wondered why there were footprints on the ceiling.

It would be a lot easier to get across this room if jetpacks were permitted in class.

Here you go, Mr. Taketo Sky.

Thanks, Sabrina.

Don't forget mine!

Now in a fashion that's **ORGANIZED**, let's form a "people line" by holding the hands of the individuals closest to you (in proximity).

This is no time to be self-consious about sweaty palms or appearing **LOVEY-DOVEY** with someone you don't find attractive! Just find a **PARTNER** and grasp on to them **AND** the concept of relying on another person to save your life!

HURRY UP AND FIND A BUDDY! We could all be dead by now if this turns out to be a **REAL EMERGENCY** instead of a simulated fake-out.

Hey, Doug.

Looks like we're partners.

If you turn out to be dead weight, I'll cut you loose without hesitation.

One at a time! Push yourselves out the door into the hallway.

The person behind you can help give support.

If only I was a forward thinker and made a **MOVE** while Sabrina was right in front of me!

Perhaps if we hadn't remained strangers it would be **MY** hand that was helping.

Still not too familiar

Based on **THE LAW OF AVERAGES** there is a good **PROBABILITY** they'll end up getting married because of this. And I'll end up depending on Doug Hiro for **EMOTIONAL SUPPORT.**

Woop Woop Woop

You guys are still alive... and that's good *SO FAR!* But here is the part of the anti-gravity drill that is even *MORE* dangerous than holding hands. You'll need to ditch your friends and go to your locker, so you can retrieve your space suits.

Done.

Once everyone

EXCEPT DOUG!

--has their suits, we'll meet again at airlock **A-3.**

Glide safely and I'll get to see you again at the rendezvous.

Wow...if I could get my mind off my broken heart...

...this might actually be exciting. *TOO BAD, I GUESS.*

Hey Maluk!

Tak! You heading to **A-3?**

Yeah, but I'm trying to find Thalia first.

I figure this might be my big chance to save her life or something cool.

Do you want us to wait for you? Then we can look for Rodney and head out into space as a team.

No, you and Thalia go ahead and live *HAPPILY EVER AFTER.*

I'd rather not be *HOVERING* in the way of true love.

I hope I'm not too depressed to remember my own locker combination.

one... ·SIGH· Such a lonely number...

KER-BLAST!

Ker-wha?

oh...

Ker-Blast!

FOOM

WATCH OUT!

My whole life just flashed before my eyes--and then you saved it!

WATCH ME!

okay...I'm watching...

But, now... you're gone!

Who was that girl?

And where did she get that adorable striped Shirt !?!

MY NAME IS: **MIYUMI SAN** みゆみ ♡♡

AND I HAVE THE POWER TO CONTROL TIME THANKS TO MR. WATCH!

It's no big.

I AM A STUDENT AT ASTRONAUT ACADEMY

Today's Adventure

Revel Without a pause.

≧Whew≦ This I.B.W. watch sure is good for slowing down and not jumping into things.

Frozen

But I still don't have enough time to explain to this bystander the details of how I came to acquire such desirable attributes.

Best to put some distance between us before things start to **ESCALATE.**

Besides, I came here looking for a **FRIEND**-- not to find myself in an **EXPLOSIVE RELATIONSHIP.**

So I hope Hakata's not hurt as badly as his defenseless locker...

...and that the video game I lent him wasn't left in there!

I knew that Hakata didn't have many friends, but never thought to ask him if he had a nemesis.

I wonder if this has anything to do with his mysterious past?

Hey! No touching!

Hakata! You're... um... messed up?

Did enough time pass for you to burn half your body then reconstruct it with artificial limbs?

Wait a **SECOND**... why aren't you waiting **MINUTES** like everyone else?

No one's supposed to move when **TIME STANDS STILL!** You're not Hakata Soy!!! You're some **IMPOSTER!** Or perhaps a long lost **BROTHER?**

SO! I guess it **WAS** only a **MATTER OF TIME.** You've discovered my identity...

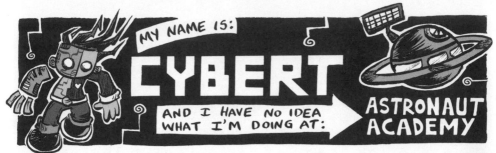

MY NAME IS:

CYBERT

AND I HAVE NO IDEA WHAT I'M DOING AT:

ASTRONAUT ACADEMY

Cybert **What?** Sounds ethnic. What are your origins?

scratchy scratchy

Well I *THOUGHT* I was programmed for **DESTRUCTION**.

But now I'm not sure.

I'm really good at blowing stuff up. Even from a distance.

But what does that *SAY* about a person?

It says "stay away from me" I think.

chop chop

Hey! You don't play Mon Chi Chi Mon do you?

I found this Charbroil Czar.

CHARBROIL CZAR

It says that he's a level 3 King Chef with Mediterranean side dish attacks.

ALSO... he's got a +3 digestive and +6 intimidation.

I'm not sure what kind of scale those are graded on. Do you have any cards I could compare stats with?

Never really got into card games. Do you mind if I leave now? You're kind of freaking me out with the obsessive personality.

Sure. Thanks for talking to me.

grasp grasp

Nice girl... Too bad she's aligned with my mortal enemy.

I guess I should detonate her locker *TOO*, just in case I *AM* still supposed to be evil.

What'd my sensors say her name was again?

SHE IS MIYUMI SAN

WHO IS ARMED WITH A WATCH THAT IS DANGEROUS TO MY MISSION AT:

Astronaut Academy

No sign of Hakata. Maybe he's already outside?

Unless he's waiting for me at **MY** locker?

And there he is! What a total waste of time I just spent. Luckily some of it was saved by Mr. Watch.

Hakata sure looks funny frozen like that.

Less sullen and more rock hard abs.

Mr. Watch, please give me the time.

Go time GO!!!

WHOA! How did you sneak up in front of me like that?

Did you know there's an evacuation?

I almost forgot!

So grab your **OUTDOOR CLOTHES** and meet me by my locker while I change into mine!

I think you might need to find **ANOTHER** space suit. One less **WEATHERED** by explosions.

BLAST!

Explosions!?!

That's what I'm talking about!

Are you okay?

I think I just had Déjà Versa... or Vice Vu...? Maybe both.

So much for me and my locker graduating TOGETHER as a team.

And now NEITHER of us have space suits or even fishbowls!

Well, well, well. If it isn't the school's cutest couple looking, WELL...

Sarcasm!?!

I should have known that my arch-rival would stoop so low.

What are you talking about in such an annoying tone of voice?

I was just going to my locker to get some gum, when I heard the sudden SOUND EFFECTS.

GUM!? Talk about lack of priorities.

Skepticism? Miyumi, I used to expect better of YOU.

This ain't lower middle-class gum used by pedestrians.

Hubble Bubble!

I don't think we've been formally introduced.

128

My name is: **Maribelle Mellonbelly**

And I have recently become a tortured soul destined to wander the lonely halls of: ASTRONAUT ACADEMY

What a coincidence! I'm **ALL ABOUT** inner turmoil! It's like my "thing."

We should totally hang out in solitude together sometime.

That is, if Miyumi doesn't mind.

My name's Hakata Soy and I'm a sadaholic.

BE CAREFUL! Her palms secrete a deadly venom.

I can't believe you have oxygen gum! I used to chew this all the time during my hero days.

Like the battle for Hoppiton?

TOSS TWIRL

You **KNOW** about that?

Let's just say a little birdie told me.

BIRD? What **KIND** of bird?

-POP-

What else did they say? Anything **SPECIFIC!?** Or defaming of character?

Did I say bird? I meant **BUNNY!** The kind with long ears and bushy tail. **TOTAL CHATTERBOX**-- like all bunnies. **RIGHT?**

Oh... You sure?

Mega sure.

I've never even <u>seen</u> a bird let alone paid attention to one.

You're better off. They just cause trouble and hold annoying grudges.

TOTALLY. I'm sans birds for life!

129

OKAY! Enough with the formalities! Can we just head to the airlock now?

Maribelle, do you mind sharing some of your gum with Miyumi?

Who, me? Of course! I ALWAYS give to charity.

Geez, thanks.

So generous of you.

It's a great tax write-off.

Darn tootin.

Brrr... Why do I feel the sudden need to shiver?

That's part of the oxygen gum's effect. It lowers your blood temperature so you can better ADAPT to the harsh realities of outer space conditions.

It also gives you thicker SKIN.
So you should be able to withstand more insults like "self-righteous tomboy."

WOOP! WOOP!

THIS ANNOUNCEMENT IS TO LET EVERYONE KNOW THAT WHAT WE THOUGHT MIGHT BE A FALSE ALARM, HAS IN FACT BEEN CONFIRMED AS A REASON TO BE ALARMED. SO, EVERYONE SHOULD BE LISTENING TO THIS OUTSIDE THE SCHOOL UNLESS THEY ARE IN TROUBLE.

EEP! I have an allergic reaction to trouble--especially the big kind (which gives me hives).

I hope we don't get marked tardy...

It's never too late to be tardy! Even to your own funeral!

HARK! There is some odd kid on the ceiling, who although a stranger... seems as *FAMILIAR* to me as my own reflection!

Well, I guess we do have similar noses.

But not for long, since yours is about to get blasted.

It will look more like a *CRATER*. And less shiny.

No need for *VIOLENT FINGER POINTING!* We were just on our way out! Right ladies?

Brrr!

NUDGE
NUDGE

AHHH...

... AAHHH...

FREAK OUT! There is no *WAY* to run without gravity.

And no one can hear you scream in space stations that are evacuated!

AHHH AHHH

CHOOO!
BLAST

DUCK!

GOOSED!

Sowwy! A'm no good at contwolling my awwergies ina cwisis!

Don't apologize. I think you just bought us a chance to escape!

A'm good of buying stuff!

≤BZZZT≤

GROSS OVERLOAD SENSORS OFF. SYSTEM REBOOT.

Caught a light *SNEEZE*, but at least they didn't ruin my precious things.

But it looks like I'll be putting the *DAMAGE* on.

Honey

We're almost to the exit thanks to my rocket boots I almost forgot I had!

Robot!

Pointer finger!

I think I'm starting to thaw...

AIRLOCK

FOOSH

If they'd stop moving it would be a lot easier to hit them.

ZAP!

So I guess I'll just shoot *RANDOMLY* and hope that something good happens.

BLAST!

AIRL

No! Not the ceiling!

ZAP!

ZAP!

Now we are **SO** trapped!

And about to be blasted!

I with I hada handkerchief.

QUICK! STAND BEHIND ME AND TAKE COVER!

Me? or her?

BOTH OF YOU!

No!

~GASP~

ZAP!

Holy smokes! How come that laser didn't fry us into scattered ashes!?

My 3-in-1 jacket is **CUSTOMIZED** with a damage-resistant nylon shell.

Like the rocket boots, compliments of my best pal, Gadget Thompson (who I wish would return my phone calls and distress signals).

I was gonna use Miyumi as a human shield, but I guess this works well enough. Oooh! And soft too!

UMMM...so if that robot keeps **FIRING AWAY**... won't the entire hallway **CAVE IN** on us?

I sure do hate it when things collapse around me.

I never imagined I'd feel the same panic as a balloon trapped indoors!

Meanwhile...

DOUG HIRO

IS floating OUTSIDE of:

ASTRONAUT ACADEMY

Just like everyone else!

Learning how to evacuate the school was probably the most stirring educational experience I've had.

If we did stuff like this every day, I could totally warm up to the academic process.

HELLO...what have we here?

So many attractive space suits.

I can't believe all these kids go to the same school as me and I never noticed them before.

A few of them actually look pretty cute.

I guess sometimes it takes seeing people *OUT OF THE USUAL CONTEXT* or gravity before you realize how *INTERESTING* they can be.

Excuse me, are those authentic C-64 air carburetors you have on?

I should have known better. Underneath the pretty exterior everyone is exactly the same.

Gross.

Empty shells with **NO APPRECIATION** for the majesty of the infinite cosmos.

They're too busy to step back from themselves and take it all in. To be engulfed in true beauty.

I don't need companionship to feel fulfillment or comfort.

I have the **WARMTH** of a billion stars...

...wrapped like a blanket
around me.

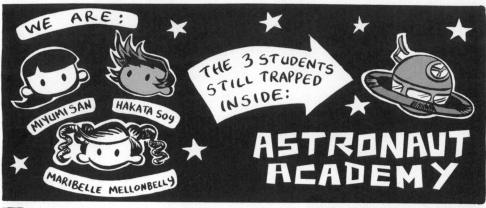

WE ARE:

MIYUMI SAN

HAKATA SOY

MARIBELLE MELLONBELLY

THE 3 STUDENTS STILL TRAPPED INSIDE:

ASTRONAUT ACADEMY

Hakata's hi-tech jacket is holding off those laser blasts, which I appreciate since I wasn't really *IN THE MOOD* to die.

ZAP!

RICOCHET!

ZAP!

It's only a matter of time before The Reaper comes to collect us all. For it is the cruel mistress "FATE" that brought us together.

SHEESH, Maribelle. I think your new wardrobe has really gone to your head, which used to be *BIG* but now is *SAD*.

Well excuse me for feeling pain that no FORCEFIELD can protect me from.

IF IT WASN'T FOR YOU I'D STILL HAVE MY BEST FRIEND AND MY NATURAL BLONDE LOCKS!

It's not *MY* fault Scab Wellington got *SENT AWAY* for detainment! Blame that *PLASTIC FORK* she wielded as a weapon without a permit.

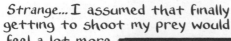

Strange... I assumed that finally getting to shoot my prey would feel a lot more emotionally satisfying.

BLAST!

And they don't seem too afflicted by my deadly assault much. I'd kind of like to just stop. But I'm not sure if it's Kosher to override my programming.

Perhaps I should consult the writings of the Guidance Chancellor. Could Bee helpful.

Bee'in yourself

DETAINMENT? You mean like prison? That means Scab is still alive! And I can probably BAIL HER OUT because I am still wealthy and well-connected!

IF Señor Panda doesn't think she's a threat to the school and my student body.

NICE COINCIDENCE! You girls stopped fighting at the same time that bipolar robot stopped trying to kill us!

What is he doing?

It LOOKS like he's reading.

We should COUNTER-ATTACK while the getting's good!

But it seems rude to interrupt someone when they are in the middle of a good book!

139

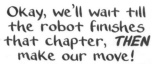

Okay, we'll wait till the robot finishes that chapter, *THEN* make our move!

But we have no *WEAPONS* and even *FISTS OF FURY* are no match for *STAINLESS STEEL CHEEKS.*

If only I had signed up for *INTRO TO ALCHEMY* instead of *CERAMICS!*

Not to sound like praise or anything *FLATTERING*... but I've seen Miyumi summon fireballs that are pretty *HOT.*

Umm... thanks for noticing?

Is that true? Do you think you can make one powerful enough to melt *METAL* into *SCRAP?*

Well, *TECHNICALLY*...

Fidget

But I need to be *REALLY UPSET* and it can be hard to control...

Leave that to an expert. If anyone knows how to push Miyumi's buttons, it's me.

Miyumi and I ARE WORST FRIENDS AT: ASTRONAUT ACADEMY

That's certainly true...

...but so far *EVEN* being trapped here with you hasn't produced enough anger or flint to get me **FIRED UP!**

Maybe we've grown *TOO MUCH* as people.

Perhaps a **FLASHBACK** will rekindle that *PAST* anger and instigate the spark we need!

You keep your flashbacks in your belly button?

Doesn't *EVERYONE?*

THINK BACK... all the way to the Bouncing Ball party I had in nursery school...

Hoo!

HA!

Remember what a bouncyfull Hoo-Ha it was?

ooh! Did you ever get to try one of those CupShakes her chef is always making all yummy?

Or bounce around on the front lawn? I always love that!

yeah.

I take it you guys have done all that stuff with her too.

Totally.

We were all in the same Pre-K investment club.

Plus my parents and Maribelle's are best friends from back in the day and also Knights.

Hey Miyumi! Did you ever go up in Mr. Mellonbelly's zepellin that looks like a Killer Whale laughing?

Um, No... I don't think so...

Oh, it's so cool. You just gotta see it.

Not as cute as Theresa's Kitten blimp.

NICE! y'all are in the same class as me!

Yeps! And so is Monique who will be late as usual.

That means the whole gang will be together!

Mind if I sit here?

Oh my gosh! Did I tell y'all about the tricked-out dinosaur my older brother bought?

No, but first you have to fill us in on the deal with that cousin of yours with the teddy bear fixation.

144

Radfastic! That was some fireball attack!

Are you okay?

You look about ten pounds lighter.

Yeah...

... it feels good to get that all out of my system.

I guess we can't still be enemies if you're my *HERO* now!

You sure!?

I mean... I couldn't have done it without you.

HUG OF SINCERITY

So now that our lives are *SAFE* should we try and open that airlock again?

Or should we clean up this mess?

I'd much rather solve the mystery behind that robot's *VENDETTA*.

WOOP WOOP

148

★ The End! ★

SCHOOL'S OUT!
But don't head home just yet....

Parent-Teacher Conferences are tonight!
Followed by the Universal Holiday Party!

Don't forget The Principal's farewell
or your epilogues!

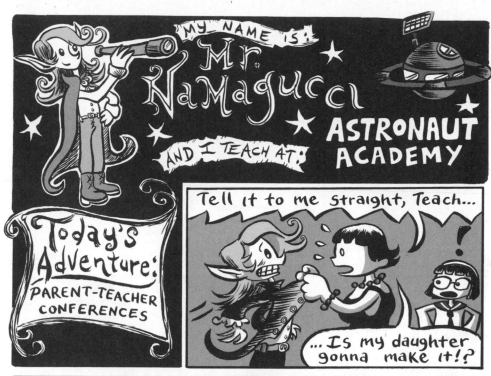

MY NAME IS Mr. Namagucci AND I TEACH AT! ASTRONAUT ACADEMY

Today's Adventure: PARENT-TEACHER CONFERENCES

Tell it to me straight, Teach...

...Is my daughter gonna make it!?

So! You're the elf my son thinks is SO smart.

STRING THEOR

E MC

GRA FOR

Just an FYI-- I'm not impressed. So save your fancy talk and twinkling for someone else.

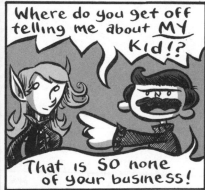

Where do you get off telling me about MY Kid!?

That is SO none of your business!

Did my children mention me at all?

It's okay if they didn't. I was hoping maybe they put in a good word for their old mom.

SCIENCE ROCKS OUT

You mean you teach "real" science?

I always assumed elves didn't believe in the stuff on account of being magic.

153

I always hoped my daughter would take *AFTER ME* and register for the I.B.W. Science Guard.

Well, you should be very proud of Thalia.

She shows tremendous skill on the field.

ERR, by which I mean the *FIELD OF SCIENCE!*

Everyone thinks she should really be the MVP.

um... Microscope Virtuoso Prodigy?

I must admit to having been concerned from time to time.

Growing up, she liked to play...

outside!

And once... I even caught Thalia watching sports on T.V. ...

...not that there's anything *WRONG* with that.

No, no, of course not.

It's perfectly natural for kids to be *CURIOUS* about competitive athletics.

Not to sound paranoid, but just between us sissies...

...Jocks frighten me.

Especially on Sundays.

PARTY TIME!

154

I really appreciate your **COVER** for my story, Mr. Namagucci.

stir

CANDY CANE

ginger lads

I won't make it a habit to deceive parents, Thalia.

Especially a high-ranking science officer who could deport me back home through the Realm Send.

And you're too good a Fireball player to keep it a secret from your dad for ever and ever.

I just do not know if he is **MATURE ENOUGH** to accept that I might not grow up in footsteps like his.

A **YOUNGER** me would have been jealous of that girl for hogging the attention of my handsomest teacher. But these past few months have made me **OLDER** and wiser.

Me too.

Oh, Grampa! You are *SO OLD* in the years past, it has become adorable to me recently.

And speaking of people of *OL'*... allow me to segue attention to my friend Molly, who you may not remember due to an absent mind.

Did she borrow my teeth once?

I'm glad you *STILL* remember old friends who were there for you *BEFORE* the enemy became so *BUDDY-BUDDY.*

MUNCH MUNCH

OVERHEAR

Just because Maribelle and I have declared a *TRUCE* it doesn't mean that our rivalry is all water under soggy bridges.

But it *DOES* mean we can now wear *MATCHING APPAREL* and not feel threatened!

156

157

SNAP!

The party continues...

So, you're **FINALLY** over Sabrina Spitaro?

It's like I **JUST** told you...

...ever since that mysterious girl popped into my line of vision, I only have **EYES** for her.

I just hope I can use them to see her again.

Well, your description isn't much to go on. There are a lot of girls who wear striped shirts and watches.

Not the way **SHE** wore stripes! Or how **SHE** checked her watch with a sense of purpose that had nothing to do with the time.

Because she **KNEW** what time it was!

Well, I say it's **TIME** for some snackage before the voyage home.

≈Sigh≈

I'll be thinking about this girl **ALL HOLIDAY BREAK** without even a name to refer to.

I know obsessing over girls you don't **KNOW** is your modus operandi...but **TRY** to practice your fling technique as well, since Fireball matches ignite the week we get back.

I wonder if she likes watching people **COMPETE?** Then maybe I could impress!

159

Great costume, Mrs. Cupcake!

Party Hat!

Thanks, Doug! You're looking pretty *FESTIVE* yourself!

SPLASH

Oh, hey! These are my parents!

Mom and Dad, this is Mrs. Cupcake, the woman I told you all about.

gesture

Well...

head Scratcher

It's nice to finally meet you *um*...face to face?

If you're wondering why they're *INVISIBLE,* it's because my folks are both bio-physicists. And they haven't figured out how to reverse the effects of their latest cloaking project.

Did they lose the ability to speak as well?

No, they gave up talking for Lent.

Hey Tak! An oldworld starcruiser just docked in the main hangar.

Might be your folks!

You going to greet them?

I *GUESS* so.

Not cuz I'm a wuss, okay? Even *HARDCORE TOUGHSTERS* have nothing to gain from leaving their parents to wander halls aimlessly.

If you say so...

SLAM

shrug

tee hee

mom dad

DASH

VISITORS

♪ OOP!

≥gulp≤

Oh! Hey, Tak... What brings you *RUNNING* down here?

Who, me? I wasn't running... I was just *EXERCISING!*

Ahh, the life of the MVP star.

Exactly.

Well if you'd like to keep your reputation *IN*, TAK, I suggest *NOT INQUIRING* about the robotic pieces in my knapsack.

Whatever you say.

Now run along before Tomcat here is forced to get his claws dirty.

Catch my drift?

Okay.

Well, have a good holiday break!

Yeah, you too!

≥whew≤ Hope he didn't suspect we were up to less good than normal for supervillains like us.

Let's hurry and find where Dad parked the vanship. I wonder if Monique is fairing better in her Maliik-spying mission *UNDER COVER* of sheets?

Mom-Mom! Pop-Pop!

Oh, my little Sourdough!

How is the eating done here? Have they fed you proper amounts of affection and ingredients?

They try.

Perhaps *NO GOOD* enough?

Thus, I bake a baguette for traveling nourishment.

MMM...I can taste home *ALREADY!* Let's get going!

Not so *QUICK*, fast guy! Let's see how this school is giving you the *SMARTS!*

I guess I *COULD* give you a little tour...I just hope no one sees us and thinks I've gone soft serve.

Oh-Kay...let's see... my locker is down that hall, near the auditorium...

Luckily it didn't *BLOW UP*, like my roommate's did. That kid has some bad luck!

Still no received messages!

≥sigh≤ What bad luck...

I guess...

...I'll be all **ALONE** for the holidays.

Hey! What happened to the Hakata Soy from a few minutes ago?

I **KNOW** he wasn't just a product of my cheerful imagination because now I have **PHOTOGRAPHIC PROOF** of his existence!

Sorry...**THAT** Hakata was picked up by his friend Gadget Thompson as was pre-arranged by my parents and his.

THIS Hakata hasn't heard from the Meta-Team, all semester.

Sounds suspiciously like you should **QUESTION** if those Gotcha Birds you speak poorly of have been **CROSSING SIGNALS** between friends and communicom devices.

SNATCH*

* FROM OFF PANEL.

My enemies were **NEVER TOO GOOD.** Especially with electronics.

They must have asked Grandma Henn to help them.

STUPID MACHINE! Doesn't understand the value of money!

Straighten the folds first!

Then let's do something similar...

...and ask **MY GRAND** to lend us a hand! He's got a **FIRM GRASP** on devices that are **HELD** in high regard.

Just wait here while I go find him.

Sure.

Not like I've got any other plans.

The end?

THE PARTY'S OVER.

I AM: THE PRINCIPAL

AND WHAT I SAY GOES AT:

ASTRONAUT ACADEMY

The educational semester has come to an end, but there is *ONE MORE* important lesson that I must impart on you before you depart.

EVIDENCE

Schools aren't always as *SAFE AS HOUSES--* especially for people without bonus lives or armor plating.

This is not just a random fact but one made more *RELEVANT* by recent revelations.

Some of you may have heard about certain events during the anti-gravity drill and started spreading *WILD RUMORS.*

And I don't blame you, for that *IS* a fun activity.

But *TRUTH* is more important than having a good time.

167

Three students (two of which were arch-rivals and one of which is a boy) were attacked in the hallway near airlock A-3.

ATTACKING is something frowned upon by people because someone may get hurt in the process.

But **SOMETIMES**...people are ROBOTS -- who may not be programmed to care.

Take it from someone who has a mechanical arm and is holding **ANOTHER** mechanical arm for emphasis...

SECURITY FOOTAGE

Robots don't go to school for a reason! They are too easily impressionable.

The one who invaded Astronaut Academy had been well-educated in the Revenging Arts.

And since that is not a subject we offer here, we can **ASSUME** that he studied abroad. Perhaps at some educational facility with a **GRUDGE**.

≥GASP!≤ If I were to jump to a **CONCLUSION** I would think that maybe our rival school had something to do with all that you are **IMPLYING!**

P.S. GAMMA Q!

Those tanuki have probably replayed that Fireball match in their minds over and over again like a record, *BROKEN* by me in the first round.

Not that I can take <u>ALL</u> the credit. Of course it was a team effort, thanks to--

IXNAY!

I mean, GO IXNAY! ALL THE WAY!

Do you have any idea what your friend is going on about?

Err... I have a hard time following anecdotal tangents.

Especially in the athletic department.

Allow us to *SHIFT ATTENTION* to the fact that Gamma Q students are also *NOTORIOUS* for their cut-throat academic aspirations!

GOOD SAVE!

And everyone is *A-BUZZ* about the inter-school talent spelling bee approaching.

Honey, don't remind me!

I wouldn't *BEE* surprised if they were trying to sting out the competition!

Them P.S. GammaQ Kids have too much hair!

YEAH!

PLUS: They don't like *ME!* Can you believe the nerve?

Your points are as **SHARP** as my educational sword of Knowledge.

And as **HEAVY!**

Thusly, this institution will **INSTITUTE** protective measures that will hopefully increase your ability to survive.

ADVANCED PLANS FOR SAFE AMOUNTS OF SECURITY.

But the Council of Elders asked that I keep these plans a secret for now. So you will have many **SURPRISES** awaiting you next semester.

So have a safe trip home, and keep a watchful eye as you **RELAX!** Come back ready for new **LEARNING SATISFACTION** with significantly less risk of robot invasion.

Happy Holidays.

THE END!

Watching the crowd shuffle away, I tried to find some last-minute *COURAGE* to do something *LOUDER* than *WIGGLE MY NOSE* like a bunny with no confidence.

There he IS! Now IS your chance to take!

≥gulp≤

All semester, I've tried to think of things to say that would make me sound like I was someone worth *KNOWING*--ya know?

MUN CHIE

And it would be so much easier if he was *JUST* some attractive boy with *UNREALISTICALLY COOL HAIR.*

But this one in particular happens to be Hakata Soy, the boy who *SAVED MY LIFE!*

I had a hard time adapting to the new **TERRAIN** of school life. The first few weeks were **ROUGH** on my feelings.

Especially the **FEET**, which were raised and lowered on **SOFT TEXTURES** like grass and soil more so than the tile and shag carpeting of space stations.

No wonder humans need shoes.

Callous

And you see, I never saw the importance of **APPEARANCES** before people started pointing out how much I don't look like them.

Ever consider laser "**HARE**" removal!?

SNARK!

And the only person who resembled me was a **TEACHER**, which is never in style.

Of course **YOU'LL** ace the test. Long-ears always look out for their **OWN** kind.

Even after I managed to make a few friends, I still longed for **HOPPIER** times.

≋Sigh≋ I'm so cooped up I feel like jumping off walls!

But then one average evening...

BAH♪ BAH BORED♪

♪ Roaming the halls again at night, might as well grab another bite. Nothing heavy, just something light. Hey! Who's that new kid, just out of sight? ♪

GASP!

The boy's dorms are down this hall.

And my R.A.'s office is right across from the study hall.

CALICO

EXTRA BLANKETS

Hakata Soy of the META TEAM!

I guess I hoped he'd recognize the medallion, or maybe even remember me.

He always looked so lost in his own thoughts and drama. I didn't have the hearts to bother him.

But just knowing that one of my role models was going to the same school gave me a renewed sense of confidence.

If you don't talk to him now, you'll regret it all winter break.

Yeah, I know.

But maybe...

...I'LL do something heroic...

...in the next two weeks.

Then when I introduce myself to him next semester, it will be as *EQUALS* rather than intergalactic hero and rural flop-eared fangirl.

How'd you lose your eye?

Battling Kraken in the depths of Tormented Space. How else?

Then can we start heading home? If we catch the right wormhole we could be back in Hoppiton by Harvest Breakfast.

All right.

Let's go.

My feet long to smoosh some topsoil again.

SEE YA NEXT SEMESTER, YOU OL' SULKY HEAD!

?

!

EPILOGUE TWO

MY NAME IS:

HAKATA SOY

はかた

AND I'M STILL HERE AT: → ASTRONAUT ACADEMY

The Gotcha Birds don't even *GO* to school. Why does The Principal think P.S. Gamma Q has anything to do with that robot who wanted to destroy us?

Things aren't always *BLACK AND WHITE* like pandas.

That's why I think the Spanish teacher will better *TRANSLATE* what we've been trying to tell people.

You sure it's okay for me to *INCONVENIENCE* your family this way?

CERTAINLY, lad! We've got an *EXTRA BEDROOM* that's been empty for the past few years lately.

And you can't pass up an opportunity to see *MY BAND* play a gig on the Original Moon, next weekend.

Maribelle even said that you can stay over at her *GUEST MANSION* once she gets home from bailing out Scab Wellington.

When we get to Earth, I'll take a closer look at this *DIGI-THINGY.*

That's very kind of you, sir!

Sir? HA! No one's called me that in *AGES* past ninety!

Miyumi, he sorta reminds me of your *LONG LOST* sister.

It's the *SPIKEY HAIR.*

My mom styled it this way.

RUFFLE

RUFFLE

Said it made me look *SHARP.*

Hey, Watawa! Seeing you *FEELS* great as always!

LICK!

I can't wait to get home so we can *CATCH* up!

This is my new friend, Hakata Soy!

BARK!

SLURP

He likes the way you taste familiar!

It's been quite a semester for school.

Thanks, Astronaut Academy, for the educational adventures! This is a good time for us to take a break!

But don't get *TOO* comfortable, because we will be back...

185

astronaut
academy
Re-Entry

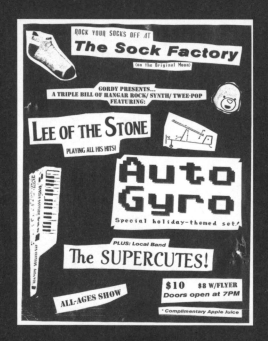

ROCK YOUR SOCKS OFF AT

The Sock Factory

(on the Original Moon)

GORDY PRESENTS...
A TRIPLE BILL OF HANGAR ROCK/ SYNTH/ TWEE-POP
FEATURING:

LEE OF THE STONE

PLAYING ALL HIS HITS!

Auto
Gyro

Special holiday-themed set!

PLUS: Local Band

The SUPERCUTES!

$10 $8 W/FLYER
Doors open at 7PM

ALL-AGES SHOW

* Complimentary Apple Juice

Gray color assists by Craig Arndt, Rosemary Travale, and Naseem Hrab. Additional crunch help from Jeremy Arambulo, Jordyn Bochon, John Green, Alisa Harris, Yuko Ota, Colleen MacIssac, Marion Vitus, and Dalton Webb.

Thanks to:

Raina Telgemeier, for making every day an awesome adventure. This book would not be possible without you.

My parents and family, for letting me get away with being a full-time cartoonist even when I was just a kid.

Chris Duffy, Laura Galen, and everyone at *Nickelodeon Magazine*, for eleven years of encouragement, inspiration, and camaraderie.

John Green, for being a great friend and comics-making teammate. Matt Hawkins, Zack Giallongo, Debbie Huey, and all my friends and fellow cartoonists who help make the world so much fun.

Everyone who was a fan and supporter of Astronaut Elementary! Tintin Pantoja, for asking me to contribute to her SVA manga anthology. Lea Hernandez and Joey Manley, for giving me an online home. Everyone at Lunchbox Funnies. Erin Houlihan, for designing the early mini-comics.

Judy Hansen, for taking even my silliest ideas so seriously.

Calista Brill, Mark Siegel, Colleen Venable, Gina Gagliano, and everyone else at First Second, for being amazing people to work with and welcoming me with such open arms.

:01

First Second
New York & London

Distributed in the United Kingdom by Macmillan Children's Books,
a division of Pan Macmillan.

Cataloging-in-Publication Data is on file at the Library of Congress.
Paperback ISBN: 978-1-59643-620-6
Hardcover ISBN: 978-1-59643-756-2

First Second books are available for
special promotions and premiums.
For details, contact: Director of Special Markets,
Holtzbrinck Publishers.

Interior book design by
Colleen AF Venable and Lawrence Lee Derks III

FIRST
EDITION

First edition 2011

Printed in March 2011 in the United States of America
by RR Donnelley & Sons Company, Crawfordsville, Indiana

Paperback 1 3 5 7 9 8 6 4 2
Hardcover 3 5 7 9 8 6 4 2

BY ART
WE LIVE